Chance

Dian Curtis Regan

Illustrated by

Dee Huxley

PHILOMEL BOOKS   NEW YORK

Library of Congress Cataloging-in-
Publication Data Regan, Dian Curtis. Chance / Dian Curtis
Regan ; illustrated by Dee Huxley.— 1st ed. p. cm.
Summary: Unhappy at home, a newborn baby packs
up his blankey and other prized possessions, leaves the farm, and
spends a year visiting and learning from bears, monkeys, sea lions,
and other creatures. [1. Babies—Fiction. 2. Animals—Fiction.
3. Voyages and travels—Fiction. 4.Home—Fiction.
5. Tall tales.] I. Huxley, Dee, ill. II. Title. PZ7.R25854
Ch 2003 [Fic]—dc21 2002001256
ISBN 0-399-23592-2
1 3 5 7 9 10 8 6 4 2
First Impression

For Garrett and Lacey Curtis
—D.C.R.

Thank you for my Chance
—D.H.

I was born in the middle of a marigold patch on a farm outside of Rosedale.

Ma'd told Pa, "Gonna chance weedin' marigolds and hope this baby don't pick today to be born."

But I did.

So . . . Pa named me Chance.

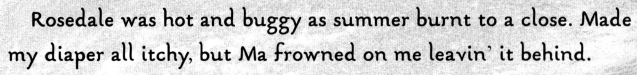

Rosedale was hot and buggy as summer burnt to a close. Made my diaper all itchy, but Ma frowned on me leavin' it behind.

She fed me gooky mush for dinner. 'Bout made me gag. Dog wouldn't even sniff it.

Pa's guitar pluckin' pained my ears and he was none too happy with my protests.

And that ol' dog? He slobbered all over my rattle. Yik!

Then Ma decided two baths a day were twice as good as one.

It all made me right cranky.

So I left.

Took a train north to cooler air, fewer bugs, and friendlier dogs.
Ended up in the mountains near Moosedale.
Met a bear gettin' his den ready for a cozy winter nap.
Said I could stay if I didn't whine and pout.

So I moved in.

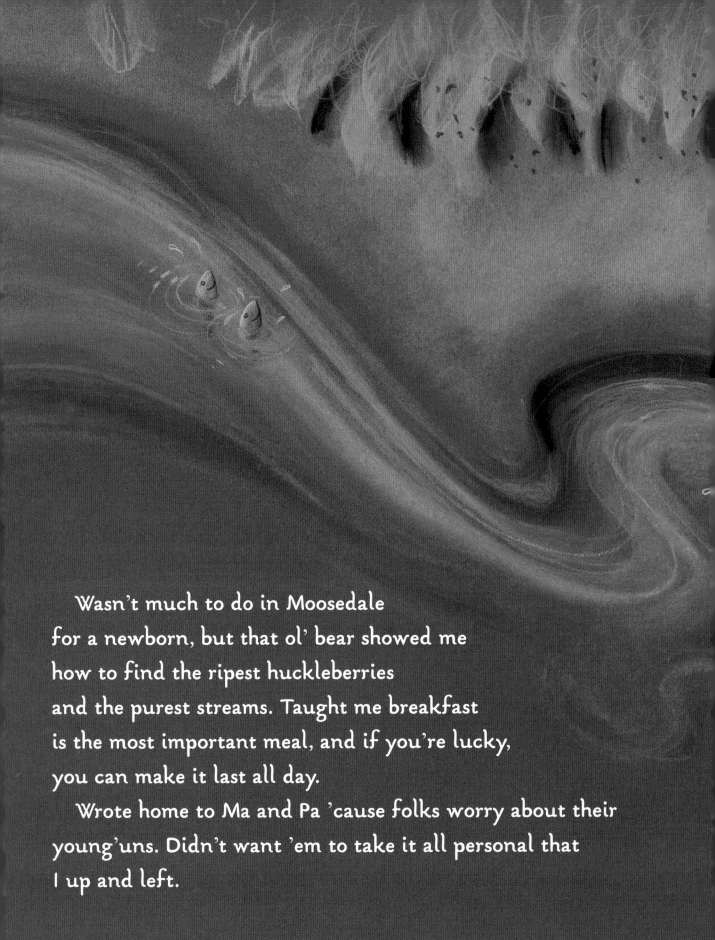

Wasn't much to do in Moosedale
for a newborn, but that ol' bear showed me
how to find the ripest huckleberries
and the purest streams. Taught me breakfast
is the most important meal, and if you're lucky,
you can make it last all day.
    Wrote home to Ma and Pa 'cause folks worry about their
young'uns. Didn't want 'em to take it all personal that
I up and left.

Ma wrote back. Said that crop of marigolds was makin' fine pots of tea. Said Pa was shooing crows from his cornstalks when his shoulder riled up and began to ache. Meant snow would come early this year.

Told me to behave and take my afternoon naps.

Made me miss Ma tuckin' me in, and the smell of that marigold tea.

Bear fell asleep and snored too loud.

Nobody to play with.

Cave, too dark.

And the nights far too nippy for my blankey.

So I left.

Took a bus to Hilldale.
Spent winter in the monkey
house at Hilldale Zoo. Monkeys taught
me how to climb, how to peel a banana,
and how to make goofy faces.
Sent the folks a photo of me and the monkeys.
Ma said I looked like Pa's side of the family. Said the
biggest blizzard in the history of Rosedale buried
the farm in snow. Pa's achy shoulder sure was right.
Told me to take at least *one* bath a day and eat my mush.
Made me miss Ma's bubbles and my pink walrus.
But not that mush.

Got right sick of bananas.
Tired of monkey antics.
Bored with folks snappin' photos all the time.
So I left.
Took a boat to Oceandale. Found a rocky beach busy with sea lions. Said I could stay if I liked to fish.

Sea lions taught me how to swim and how to bark in complete sentences. Taught me to take turns on the slide and not quibble over my share of snacks.

Spent the spring watchin' mama seals with their pups, barkin'
songs to the sea. Made me downright lonely. Started to
miss Pa's guitar pluckin' on those three flat strings.

Missed Ma's laugh so much, I called home 'stead of
writin'—just to hear it one more time.

Ma was right proud to hear her li'l Chance talkin' so well.
Told me Pa's ol' dog's been mopin' since I left. Said careful
not to swallow fish bones and don't take a dip after eatin'.

Rains came. Beach got soggy. Didn't bother them sea lions.
Bothered me.

So I left.

Caught a ride to Stonedale. Found a cool cave near a tall cactus.

Rabbit taught me how to tell a weed from a tasty marigold.

Lizard taught me to stay in the shade when the sun's beatin' down hot and shimmery.

Hawk taught me how to tell tomorrow's weather by lookin' at tonight's sky.

Wrote home to tell Pa he didn't need aches and pains for readin' the weather no more. Not with the sky spellin' it all out for him.

Ma wrote back. Said it was nigh time to plant her marigold patch again. Said that ol' dog's been sleepin' in my crib like he's missin' me much as she is.

Then Ma said, "I love you."

Made me feel like I'd choked on a whole bowl of them fish bones.

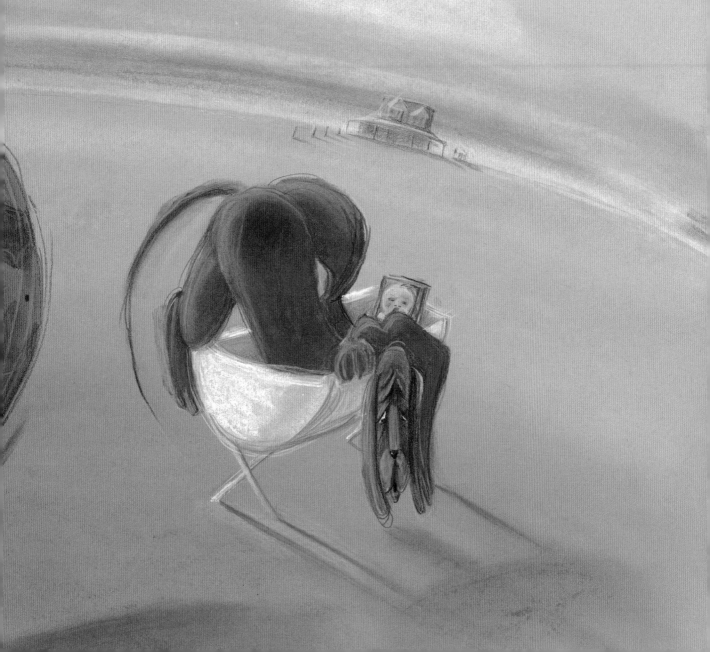

Ma said if I'd think on comin' home, she'd bake me the sweetest birthday cake Rosedale ever saw. Said she'd spoon on chocolate frostin' thick as a pumpkin stem. Sprinkle peppermint candies on top.

Made a tear wet my lash to think of that ol' dog a-sleepin' in my crib.

Called home. Said, "No more gooky supper mush?"

"No," Ma told me. "You're big enough for solid food now."

Thought about travelin' back to the mountains to visit that bear. Then on to say "Howdy" to those monkeys. Thought them seal pups might need checkin' on.

But how could I miss my own first birthday? Or a cake with peppermint candies? What if Ma needed help tellin' marigolds from weeds, or peeling bananas? What if Pa needed someone who could fish like a sea lion and bark loud enough to scare crows from his cornstalks?

What if they both were hankerin' to learn how to make goofy faces?

Most of all, sounded like that ol' dog needed a good huggin'. And only I could teach him how to make breakfast last all day.

Me? I reckon I miss the folks as much as I miss that dog. Maybe it's time to give 'em all another chance.

Guess I'll pack up my blankey, horsey, and rattle. Then head on back to Rosedale.

It's hot and buggy this time of year. . . .

But it's home.